OBADIAH THE BOLD

OBADIAH

PUFFIN BOOKS

the BOLD

STORY AND PICTURES BY

Brinton Turkle

PUFFIN BOOKS

Viking Penguin Inc., 40 West 23rd Street, New York, New York 10010, U.S.A.
Penguin Books Ltd, 27 Wrights Lane, London W8 5TZ (Publishing & Editorial) and
Harmondsworth, Middlesex, England (Distribution & Warehouse)
Penguin Books Australia Ltd, Ringwood, Victoria, Australia
Penguin Books Canada Limited, 2801 John Street, Markham, Ontario, Canada L3R 1B4
Penguin Books (N.Z.) Ltd, 182–190 Wairau Road, Auckland 10, New Zealand

First published by The Viking Press 1965
Viking Seafarer Edition published 1969
Published in Picture Puffins 1977
Reissued 1988
Copyright © Brinton Turkle, 1965
All rights reserved
Printed in Japan by Dai Nippon Printing Co. Ltd.
Set in Garth

Library of Congress Cataloging in Publication Data
Turkle, Brinton.   Obadiah the Bold.
Summary: A young boy's desire to be a pirate is
quelled by his brothers and sisters during a game.
[1. Friends, Society of—Fiction]   I. Title.
PZ7.T8470b7   [E]   77–4163   ISBN 0-14-050233-5

For Jonathan

This is Obadiah Starbuck. He is running home with his new spyglass. It is made of brass and it is very beautiful.

The rest of his family, all dressed in their best clothes, are going to Friends Meeting: Father, Mother, Moses, Asa, Rebecca, and Rachel. Obadiah comes between Rebecca and Rachel. The beautiful new spyglass was a birthday present. When Obadiah tried to take it to Meeting, Father said, "No," and Obadiah had to run back home with it.

On First Day, all the Quakers on Nantucket Island go to Meeting. There the men sit on one side and the women sit on the other. When Obadiah arrived, Meeting had already begun. He sat on a wooden bench with the men.

Meeting for Worship was long and quiet. Sometimes a Friend would stand up and recite verses from the Bible or talk about God. Obadiah tried to think about God, but it was easier to think about his shiny new spyglass. A fly buzzed on the sunny windowpane. All of a sudden, Obadiah knew what he wanted to be when he grew up.

He wanted to be a pirate. He wanted to be a fearless pirate who roamed the seas and had chests of treasure buried in secret places. Obadiah Starbuck, Terror of the Seven Seas! OBADIAH THE BOLD!

If Obadiah's new spyglass couldn't go to Meeting, it went every place else with him: to the wharf, to bed . . .

and even to the table at mealtimes.

"When I grow up, I'm going to be a pirate," he said at suppertime.

Moses whooped. "Has thee ever heard of a Quaker pirate?" he asked Asa.

"Perhaps he could be a Friendly pirate," said Mother. Everyone laughed.

Father said, "I don't think a Starbuck has ever been a pirate, Obadiah; but if that is thy heart's desire, I hope thee will be a good one."

One rainy day Rachel asked him to play house with her.

"No!" Obadiah snorted. "I am too big to play house with thee."

In the parlor Moses and Asa had just filled the woodbox. Rebecca was sweeping the hearth.

"Let's play pirate," he suggested.

"All right," said Asa. "First, Moses and I capture thee!" They were bigger than he was and there were two of them. Rebecca got some rope and a piece of cloth. Obadiah was tied and blindfolded.

"We're putting thee in the brig," they said.

"That's not the way to play pirate!" shouted Obadiah.

"It is too!" they said. They put him in the broom closet and shut the door.

Pirates are brave and don't cry. But Obadiah was frightened and wanted very much to cry. He tried to push his way out of the closet, but someone was holding the door.

"Avast there, mate! Shall we keelhaul this dog, or hang him from the yardarm?"

That didn't sound like Moses.

"No, we'll send him down to Davy Jones. Get out the plank."

That didn't sound like Asa.

There was a scuffling sound and at last the door was opened. He was pushed and shoved until he was standing unsteadily on some kind of board.

"March!" someone said.

He didn't budge.

"Jab him with a harpoon!"

Something poked him in the ribs and he had to jump.

He was surprised to find himself on the floor. Rebecca took off the blindfold and untied him. The plank was only a board from the woodshed. The harpoon must have been the broom handle.

Moses and Asa were laughing. Obadiah didn't think it was funny.

The rest of the afternoon, he played house with Rachel.

That night he didn't take his spyglass to the supper table. He didn't even take it to bed with him.

The next day Obadiah walked back and forth three times in front of Father's study before Father looked up from the letter he was writing and said, "Come in, son."

Obadiah stood stiffly beside the desk and didn't know how to begin.

"Is anything troubling thee?" Father asked.

"Father, is it true that pirates have to walk the plank?"

"Why, yes, if they're caught."

"And must they hang from the yard-arm?"

"If they're wicked enough."

"Then...then I don't want to be a pirate no matter how brave they are."

Father picked Obadiah up and sat him on his knee. "Pirates aren't really very brave, Obadiah," he said. "I never heard of a pirate as brave as thy own grandfather."

"What did he do?"

"He sailed around the Horn four times."

"What's the Horn, Father?"

"Cape Horn is land's end at the very tip of South America. Thee has to go around it to get to the China Seas, and it is very dangerous."

"Why?"

"Because there are rocks and ice and foul weather. Terrible storms blow down there. Twice thy grandfather was almost ship-wrecked, but he brought his ship through and never lost a man. He was such a brave sailor that his men gave him a fine gift."

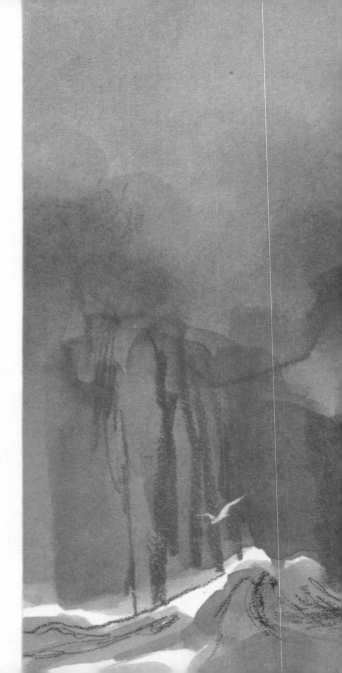

"What was it?"

"I'll show it to thee." Father went over to the high chest in the corner. From the top drawer, he brought out a red box which he opened. Inside was the most beautiful thing Obadiah had ever seen.

"A watch!"

"It's like a watch, son, but it's especially for sailors. It's called a *chronometer*. It keeps very accurate time, and that helps to tell exactly where thy ship is at sea. Pick it up and look at it."

Obadiah picked it up with great care.

Father said, "Turn it over and look on the back."

There was writing on the back. Obadiah couldn't read the letters very well, but one word almost jumped out at him.

"OBADIAH!" he yelled. "It's my name!"

Father took the chronometer and held it up to the window where it twinkled, crystal and gold in the light. "For Obadiah Starbuck," he read. "Brave Captain of the ship *Bonaventure* from the ship's company. 1798."

"That's my name!"

"Thee was named for thy grandfather, Obadiah. I think he would want thee to have this timepiece when thee is a man. I'll put it away for now." Father returned it to the chest drawer. "It's a fine day, son. Go get thy spyglass and come up to the roof with me."

It *was* a fine day. In Nantucket harbor a whaling ship was rolling at anchor as if she wanted to get under way. Beyond the breakwater a far-off ship was headed for Boston.

"Which way is the Horn, Father?"

"Away off yonder," Father said, pointing.

"Farther than France?"

"Much farther."

"Someday I'll see it," said Obadiah.

Father put his hand on Obadiah's shoulder.

"I expect thee will," he said.